USBORNE

00649887

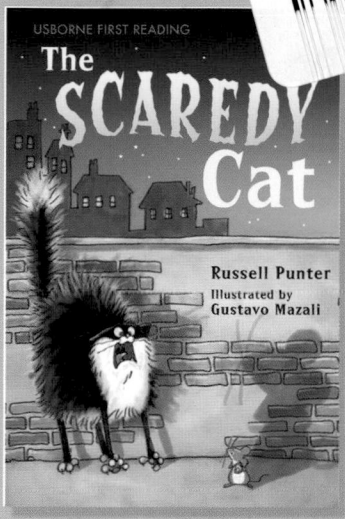

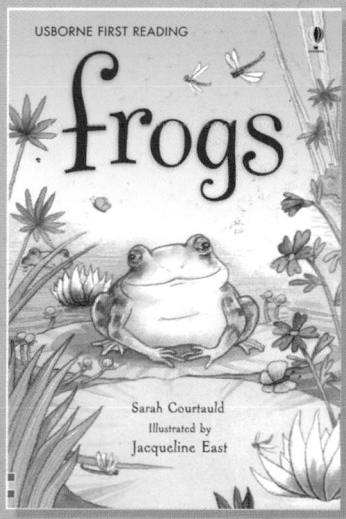

Thumbelina

Based on a story by
Hans Christian Andersen

Retold by
Susanna Davidson

Illustrated by Petra Brown

Reading Consultant: Alison Kelly
Roehampton University

Once, there was a woman who wanted a child.

She wanted one more than anything else in the world.

At last, she went to a fairy for help.

"Here is a magic seed," said the fairy.

"Put it in a flower pot, and see what happens."

The seed grew into a beautiful red-gold flower.

The woman bent and kissed it.

And the petals of the flower began to open.

Inside was a tiny girl, no bigger than a thumb.

The woman made her a bed out of a walnut shell. It had rose petals for sheets.

Each day, Thumbelina floated on a tulip leaf in a saucer of water.

When she felt lonely, she sang to herself.

One night, a large, lumpy toad crept through the open window...

She snatched Thumbelina as she slept.

"What a pretty wife you'll make for my son," she croaked.

Her son grinned and gazed at Thumbelina, happily.

"We'll keep her on a water lily in the middle of the stream," said Mother Toad.

"She'll never escape."

Thumbelina woke to see four large eyes, blinking at her.

Then a large webbed hand reached for her.

"No!" cried Thumbelina,
trying to get away.

"Meet your future
husband," said Mother Toad.

"But I don't want to marry a toad," Thumbelina sobbed.

The fishes in the stream heard her cries.

The toads left for food and the fish swam closer.

They nibbled and nibbled at the water lily.

And it was swished away by the stream.

Thumbelina floated for days, past villages and wide green fields.

Butterflies fluttered around her. Birds twittered and sang to her.

The sun shone on the water so that it glittered like gold.

But, all the time, a big brown beetle was watching her.

He swooped down and grabbed her in his claws.

"Yuck!" said the lady beetles. "She's ugly. Take her away!"

So the beetle dropped her in a field.

For tiny Thumbelina, the field was like a forest.

There she lived, all summer.

She wove herself a bed with blades of grass, and hung up a leaf to stop the rain.

She sucked honey from flowers and drank the dew from their leaves.

Swallows swooped and dived around her, so she never felt alone.

Then winter came and the swallows left. Thumbelina shivered with cold.

"What are you doing out here?" asked a field mouse.

She took Thumbelina back to her snug little home.

"We'll have a visitor soon," said the field mouse. "He's a rich and clever mole."

When the mole came, he talked about his life underground.

"I never go outside," he said. "Come and see my splendid house."

Thumbelina went with him down a dark tunnel.

In the middle of the tunnel lay a bird. He had fallen through a hole in the roof.

"Oh! Is he dead?" asked Thumbelina.

"Yes," replied Mole. "If swallows don't fly away for winter, they die of cold."

That night, Thumbelina crept back to the swallow.

She covered him with a carpet of hay.

"Goodbye!" she said, thinking how sweetly the swallows sang all summer.

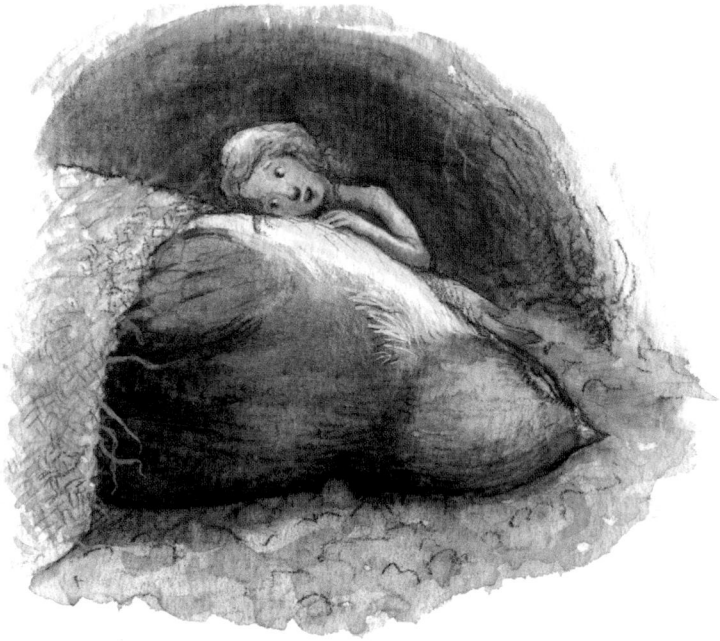

But when she put her head on his breast, she heard a, "*Thump*! *Thump*! *Thump*!"

"He's not dead. He's frozen," she realized.

The next night, Thumbelina crept back to see the bird again.

His eyes were open, but he was very weak.

"I'll keep you warm and take care of you," said Thumbelina.

"Thank you," whispered the swallow.

Each night, Thumbelina brought him water and seeds from the field mouse's store.

By springtime, when the sun warmed the earth, the swallow was well again.

"Come with me," he said. "We can fly away to the green woods."

"I can't," said Thumbelina. "I think the field mouse would be sad if I left."

So the swallow flew up out of the tunnel and soared into the sky, alone.

Thumbelina missed the swallow. She longed to go outside again.

"Cheer up!" said the field mouse. "I have exciting news. Mole wants to marry you."

"But I don't want to marry Mole," gasped Thumbelina.

"Nonsense!" snapped the field mouse. "Don't be difficult."

The wedding day was fixed. Thumbelina was to live deep under the earth.

She went to say goodbye to the sky one last time.

"Tweet, tweet," she heard. She looked up and saw the swallow.

"Cold winter is coming again," he said. "Come with me to warmer countries."

"Oh, I'll come, I'll come!" cried Thumbelina.

She climbed on his back.
They flew high, over forests
and seas and snow-covered
mountains.

At last, they came to a blue lake. A dazzling white palace stood on its sunny shore.

The swallow set Thumbelina down in a large white flower.

A tiny man stood in the flower. He had a gold crown and pale butterfly wings.

He took off his crown and gave it to Thumbelina.

"Will you stay with me and be Queen of the Flowers?" he asked.

"Yes," said Thumbelina, happy at last.

Then all the other flowers opened and tiny men and women appeared.

They each gave Thumbelina a gift.

Best of all was a beautiful pair of wings, so she could fly from flower to flower.

And the swallow swooped above them all, singing a joyful song.

Thumbelina was first told by Hans Christian Andersen, who was born in Denmark in 1805. He said he heard this story from a swallow, who had a nest outside the window of his house in Denmark. The swallow came to him one summer and sang him the story.

Designed by Jessica Johnson
Series designer: Russell Punter
Series editor: Lesley Sims

First published in 2008 by Usborne Publishing Ltd., Usborne House, 83-85 Saffron Hill, London EC1N 8RT, England. www.usborne.com
Copyright © 2008 Usborne Publishing Ltd.

All rights reserved. No part of this publication may be reproduced, stored in a retrieval system or transmitted in any form or by any means, electronic, mechanical, photocopying, recording or otherwise, without the prior permission of the publisher. The name Usborne and the devices are Trade Marks of Usborne Publishing Ltd.
Printed in China. UE. First published in America in 2009.

USBORNE FIRST READING
Level Four

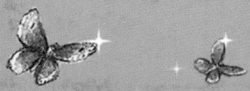